Monster
Stew

MITRA MODARRESSI

A DK INK BOOK
DK PUBLISHING, INC.

In loving memory of my father
Taghi Modarressi

DK
Ink

DK Publishing, Inc., 95 Madison Avenue, New York, New York 10016
Visit us on the World Wide Web at http://www.dk.com

Library of Congress Cataloging-in-Publication Data
Modarressi, Mitra
Monster stew / written and illustrated by Mitra Modarressi. — 1st ed.
p.   cm.
Summary: Presents three fairy tales, based on themes from traditional tales
and Hans Christian Andersen, featuring a variety of monsters.
ISBN 0-7894-2517-3   [1. Fairy tales. 2. Monsters—Fiction.]   I. Title.
PZ7.M7137Mo   1998   [E]—dc21 97-39418 CIP   AC

Book design by Jennifer Browne.
The illustrations for this book are watercolor on Fabriano paper.
The text of this book is set in 14 point Stempel Garamond.
Printed and bound in U.S.A.

First Edition, 1998
2 4 6 8 10 9 7 5 3 1

Stoddart
K😊ds

Published in Canada in 1998 by Stoddart Kids, a division of Stoddart Publishing Co. Limited,
34 Lesmill Road, Toronto, Canada M3B 2T6

Distributed in Canada by General Distribution Services,
30 Lesmill Road, Toronto, Canada M3B 2T6

Tel (416) 445-3333   Fax (416) 445-5967   E-mail Customer.Service@ccmailgw.genpub.com
ISBN (Canada): 0-7737-3106-7
Information available from Cataloguing in Publication Data (Canada).

Contents

Once there was a prince named Thugmond who was his parents' pride and joy. Nothing was ever too good for their son.

One day Thugmond told the king and queen, "I would like to get married."

They were delighted. "We must find you a princess."

But Thugmond already had someone in mind—his very best friend, Griselda. His parents were dismayed to hear this. "Certainly not!" said the queen.

"She's no princess!" said the king.

Thugmond was disappointed. In his eyes, Griselda would make a perfect wife. They both loved romping with their pet lizards and picking toadstools in the royal caves, and they always had fun together. But it was true, Thugmond sadly admitted, "She's not a princess."

"Don't worry, son. We shall find you one," promised the king.

As they were the only royalty in the area, the king and queen wrote to kingdoms far and wide, hoping a princess would respond. Finally one did. They invited her to visit right away.

The glorious day came at last. But when Thugmond met the princess at the castle gate, he was shocked! There stood a dainty, delicate girl with golden hair and a gown of silk and satin. Not Thugmond's type at all. His parents looked worried, and so did the princess.

"Shall we walk in the garden?" Thugmond asked politely. The princess agreed. He showed her all of his favorite plants, but she did not seem to like them.

She didn't even admire
his bug collection.

At dinner she barely touched her plate. "What kind of a princess doesn't enjoy a good swamp stew?" wondered the queen.

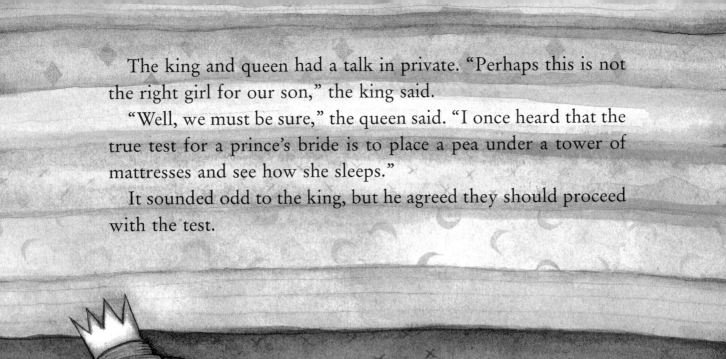

The king and queen had a talk in private. "Perhaps this is not the right girl for our son," the king said.

"Well, we must be sure," the queen said. "I once heard that the true test for a prince's bride is to place a pea under a tower of mattresses and see how she sleeps."

It sounded odd to the king, but he agreed they should proceed with the test.

The next morning, when the very cranky-looking princess came downstairs, they asked her, "How did you sleep?"

"Dreadfully!" the princess snapped. "I'm black and blue all over. It's as if I'd been lying on a bed of rocks." And with that she stomped out the door.

"My word! And all because of a tiny pea," said the queen. "A girl so rude and fussy could never make Thugmond happy."

"Indeed!" agreed the king. "The pea has proven this girl to be unworthy."

Again Thugmond asked, "Couldn't I maybe marry Griselda?"

This time his parents thought it over.

"Well," said the king, "if Griselda can pass the test that the princess failed, then she is good enough for our son." And so she was invited for a weekend.

Griselda was delighted, for she had been smitten with Thugmond for as long as she could remember. She arrived at the castle in her best outfit. Thugmond was pleased.

They spent the afternoon fishing in the swamp.

Then they joined the king and queen for dinner. "She's a little wild," the queen whispered to the king.

"Yes, but such a healthy appetite!" said the king.

When it was bedtime, they showed Griselda to her room. "Now we shall see if she's right for our Thugmond," the king told the queen.

Griselda was thrilled to see the mountain of mattresses. She wasn't at all sleepy, so she climbed the steep, steep bed . . .

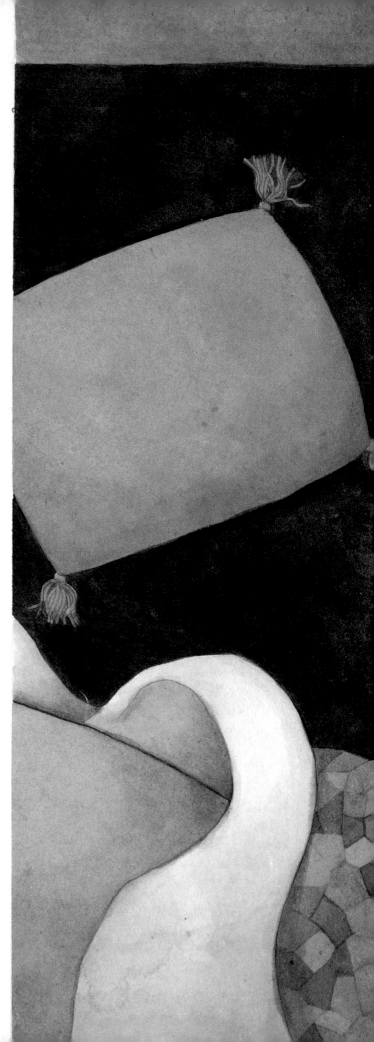

. . . and jumped up and down and up and down until she almost reached the ceiling.

At last, when she was worn out, Griselda crawled under the covers and fell happily asleep.

The next morning when Griselda bounded downstairs, the king asked, "And how did you sleep?"

"Like a log!" she answered truthfully. The king and queen rejoiced. She hadn't felt the pea at all. This was the girl for Thug-mond!

"So polite!" the queen said.

"So good-natured!" the king approved.

"So sturdy!" Thugmond glowed.

And so it was with his parents' blessing that Thugmond asked Griselda to marry him. She gladly accepted, and together they lived happily ever after.

Beans

Once there was a grumpy giant monster who lived in a castle high in the clouds. He spent his time counting his riches and guarding them from burglars.

One day he noticed that a bag of coins was missing. "Dratted thieves!" he growled. He tore through the castle, but found no one.

For several days he sulked about his lost bag of coins. To soothe his nerves, he decided that he would play his golden harp. But when he went to the cupboard, it was gone. "Curses!" he roared. "Who dares to steal my treasures?" He turned the castle upside down, but saw no sign of the thief.

The monster was determined that this would not happen again. So he set his prize goose that laid golden eggs out on the table and pretended to doze off.

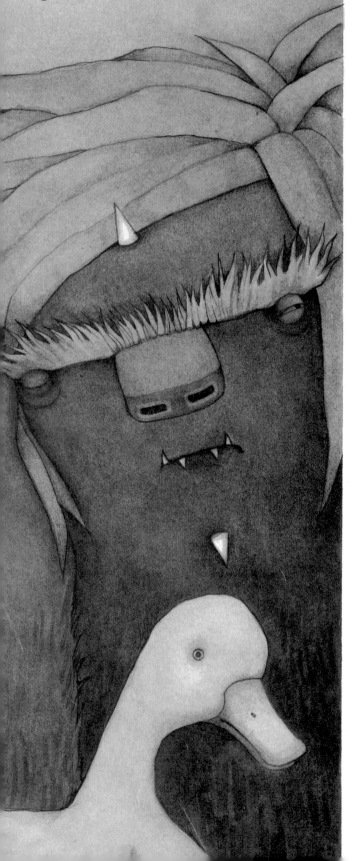
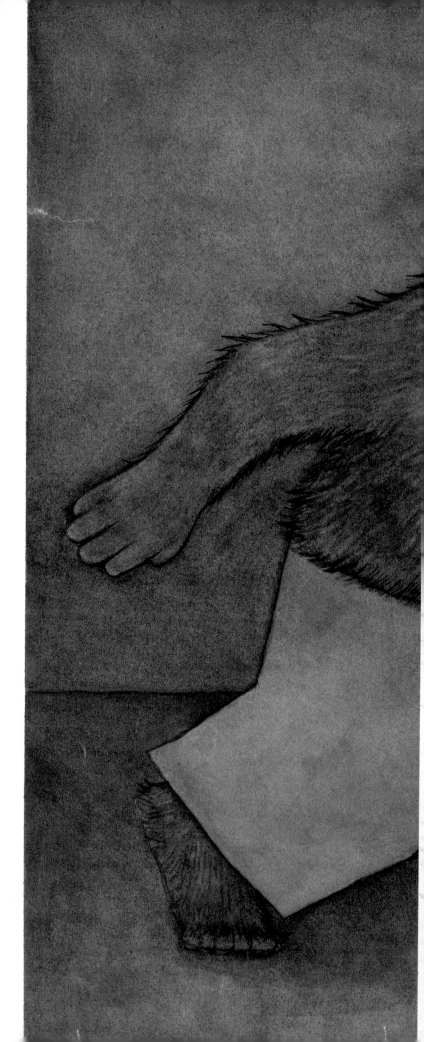

Sure enough, a little boy tip-toed out and grabbed the goose. *"Squawk!"* went the goose, and the monster leapt to his feet. He was astonished to see such a small creature. "Aha!" he thundered. The little boy yelped and took off as fast as he could. "Halt!" the monster cried. "Unhand my goose!" The ground shook as he lumbered after the boy.

The monster chased the boy out of the castle to a huge bean-stalk that he'd never seen before. Down they went. The little boy reached the ground first and cried out, "Mama! Bring the ax!" The boy and his mother began to chop at the stalk.

With a loud bellow the monster thudded to the ground, along with the beanstalk. When he opened his eyes, he saw two terrified little people backing away from him. "Ouch! My arm!" moaned the monster.

The mother stopped in her tracks. "Wait, Jack. I think he's hurt. We can't just leave him here." They crept toward him and peered down at his face.

"Oh, the pain," the monster whined.

The mother took another step forward and said, "I'm Mrs. Rumple, and this is my son, Jack. Are you hurt?"

"Well, of course I'm hurt!" the monster snapped. "Not only that, but I'm missing one bag of coins, one golden harp, and my goose that lays golden eggs!"

"Jack!" gasped Mrs. Rumple. "Have you been stealing?"

Jack hung his head in shame. "We were so poor, Mother," he said, "and we've had such a hard time keeping up the farm on our own."

"That's no excuse. You apologize this minute!" she ordered.

Jack turned to the monster. "I'm sorry," he said. "I traded our cow for some magic beans. When they grew into a beanstalk that reached your kingdom, I couldn't resist taking a few things for my poor mother."

"Well, what am I supposed to do now?" the monster muttered. "You've chopped down the beanstalk, so how am I going to get home again?"

"Why don't you stay with us for a while?" Mrs. Rumple offered. "You're in no shape to travel anyhow."

"Well, if I must," the giant grunted.

Jack and his mother helped the monster into their cottage and made a bed for him by the fire. He had to admit it was very cozy. Mrs. Rumple brought him homemade soup and patched his cuts and soothed his bruises with ointment.

"Why, this is rather nice," the monster thought to himself. Jack kept him company and entertained him with stories. As time passed, the monster grew a little bit fond of the Rumples. Soon his bruises healed, but every day he put off leaving. And every day, Jack and his mother said, "Oh, don't go just yet."

The monster even started to help out around the farm. To his surprise, he found he enjoyed himself. The farm was once again a success, and Jack and his mother were grateful. "Won't you stay with us always?" they asked. "We've grown to love you dearly."

The monster realized that he felt the same about them. "Well, I suppose I could stay," he said gruffly, and the three of them lived happily ever after.

—34—

Monster Stew

Once upon a time there were two small monsters, Hansel and his sister, Gretel.

One day they set out for a stroll in a nearby forest. Deeper and deeper into the woods they went, munching on fruits and berries and an occasional tree as they walked, until they came across a beautiful gingerbread house. "Oh, what luck!" said Gretel. And they dug right in, for monsters have quite an appetite.

The house belonged to a wicked witch, and she was watching them from behind a tree. "I was hoping to catch some plump little children," she thought to herself, "but these monsters will do nicely. I'll fatten them up and eat them for Sunday supper."

The witch stepped out from her hiding place. "Welcome, dearies," she said in her friendliest voice. "You seem so hungry. Won't you stay for lunch?"

"Oh, thank you!" said Gretel between chomps.

"We're famished," said Hansel.

The witch cooked them a feast. "I hope you like it," she said, and indeed they did, for they ate every last bite, including the plates and the silverware and the flowers on the table.

The witch thought they were a bit piggish, but she was sure that they would taste delicious. "Wouldn't you like to rest for a while?" she offered.

Hansel and Gretel accepted. She showed them to the cellar and locked the door behind them. "What a lovely hostess!" said Hansel.

"Yes," agreed Gretel. "And such a nice home!"

As the monsters napped, the witch looked through her cookbooks. "I must find a good monster stew recipe," she cackled.

But Hansel and Gretel didn't sleep for long. "I'm starving," said Gretel.

"Me, too," said Hansel. "Let's eat!" And they began to gnaw their way through the cellar. They ate three bags of apples, two bags of flour, a ball of string, a pile of firewood, seven pairs of old shoes, and a bicycle.

"What's all that racket?" the witch yelled down to the cellar.

"We're hungry!" cried Hansel and Gretel.

"All right," the witch answered, "I'll get you a snack."

Instead she went out to her garden to gather ingredients for
the monster stew. By now Hansel and Gretel had eaten the
entire basement, but they were still hungry, so they ate
straight through the cellar door and started chewing
on the kitchen.

"You beasts!" the witch cried when she came in. "You're eating me out of house and home!"

"But we're *starving*!" Hansel said.

"Did you get more treats?" asked Gretel.

"All in good time," the witch said, and she shooed them out of the kitchen. She realized that she had better make her monster stew quickly, while she still had a kitchen left. She put her biggest kettle on the stove and started chopping vegetables.

Hansel and Gretel tried to behave, but they were just too hungry. By the time the witch came to get them, Gretel had swallowed four jars of potion and three flying broomsticks, and Hansel had finished off the witch's library of spell books and her magic wand.

"Fiends!" the witch screeched.

They tried to apologize, but eating all that magic made Hansel hiccup fireflies, and Gretel kept floating off the ground.

"You two are impossible!" the witch said. "Kabloo-kablon, be gone!" And she waved her arms, but nothing happened. "Oh, no!" she cried. "Where's my wand? I'm ruined!" And she hopped on her only remaining broomstick and fled.

Hansel and Gretel waved good-bye, and after polishing off the rest of the house, they decided to head for home.